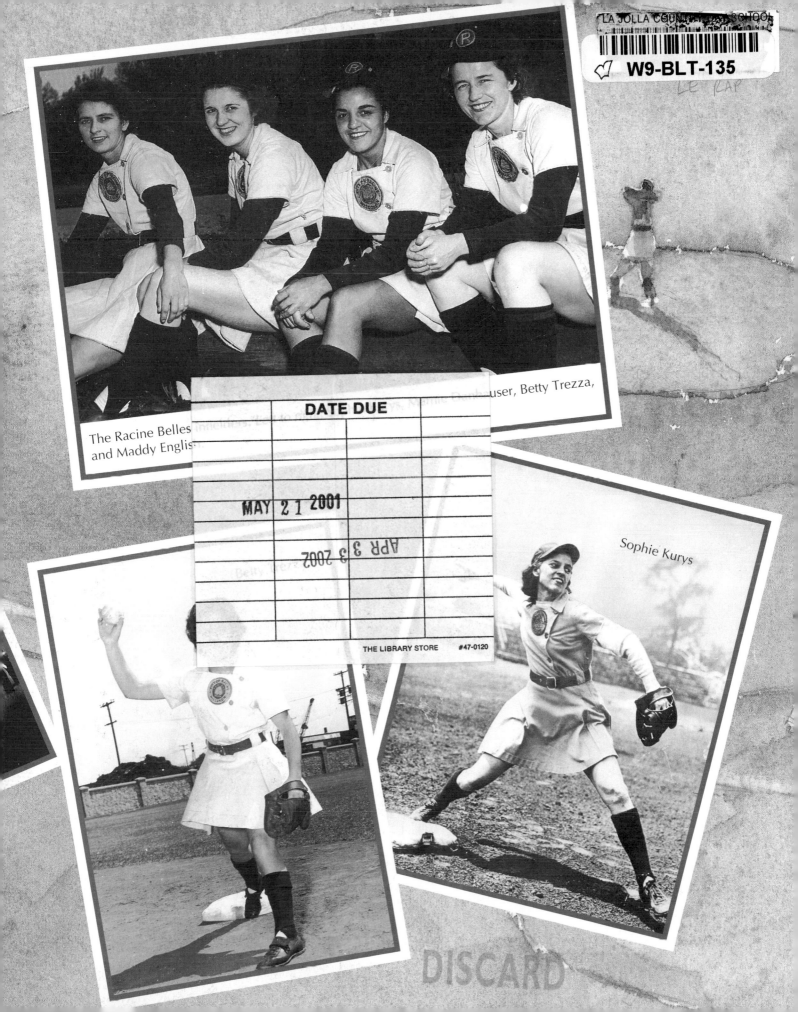

The Racine Belles ... ... Mattie Denhauser, Betty Trezza, and Maddy Englis...

Sophie Kurys

# Dirt on Their Skirts

# Dirt on Their Skirts

## THE STORY OF THE YOUNG WOMEN WHO WON THE WORLD CHAMPIONSHIP

Doreen Rappaport
Lyndall Callan

PICTURES BY
E. B. Lewis

Dial Books for Young Readers · New York

Published by Dial Books for Young Readers
A division of Penguin Putnam Inc.
345 Hudson Street
New York, New York 10014

Designed by Nancy R. Leo-Kelly
Printed in Hong Kong on acid-free paper
First Edition
1 3 5 7 9 10 8 6 4 2

Library of Congress Cataloging in Publication Data
Rappaport, Doreen.
Dirt on their skirts: the story of the young women who won the world championship/
by Doreen Rappaport and Lyndall Callan; pictures by E. B. Lewis.
p. cm.
Summary: Margaret experiences the excitement of watching the 1946 championship game of
the All-American Girls Professional Baseball League as it goes into extra innings.
ISBN 0-8037-2042-4
[1. All-American Girls Professional Baseball League—Fiction. 2. Baseball—Fiction.]
I. Callan, Lyndall. II. Lewis, Earl B., ill. III. Title.
PZ7.R18135Di 2000 [Fic]—dc21 98-47080 CIP AC

*The full-color artwork was prepared using watercolors.*

✦ ✦ ✦

*For the Berkshires women's group and its outstanding teamwork*
D.R.

*To my four mothers—all strong women*
L.C.

*To the Princeton Day School, thanks for your participation*
E.B.L.

Margaret slurped the last drop of soda from her second bottle of pop. But her throat still felt dry and tight from yelling for the past two and a half hours. The championship game between her home team, the Racine Belles of Wisconsin, and the Rockford Peaches of Illinois, had not been settled in the usual nine innings. It was now the bottom of the fourteenth and the score was still frozen at 0-0.

"Are the Belles ever going to get a run?" Margaret pleaded.

"Soon," her mother said.

Margaret didn't think she could wait much longer.

One run in this inning would make the Belles the 1946 champions of the All-American Girls Professional Baseball League. The league had been formed three years before when the United States was at war. Margaret, her mother and brother, Robert, had gone to every home game. Margaret had mailed the scorecards to her father, who had been fighting overseas. The war was over now, and her father joined them at the games.

Joanne Winter was at bat. Robert thought she was the best pitcher in the league, and she had the awards to prove it. Joanne had two strikes against her.

"Put it over the outfield wall!" Robert called.

"Send it overseas!" yelled Margaret's father.

Horlick Field was packed with shouting fans. Margaret's family had come early to make sure they got seats. People who hadn't were sitting on the grass by the outfield wall.

The pitch ripped toward home plate. Joanne swung and missed.

"Strike three!"

Now there was one out.

Margaret added another "K" to her scorecard to indicate a strikeout. She felt chilly, so she borrowed her mother's jacket to drape over her legs.

"Hide those scabby knees," teased Robert.

"You have to be tough to play baseball in a skirt," countered their mother.

Margaret didn't mind dirt on her skirt or scrapes and bruises. It was all part of playing baseball—the sting on her legs when she slid into home plate or the ache in her throwing arm after a game. One day Margaret hoped to play second base for the Belles, like her favorite player, Sophie Kurys.

"The Flash is up," Robert said.

Sophie Kurys stepped up to the plate. Her nickname was "The Flint Flash." "Flint," for Flint, Michigan, her hometown, and "Flash" for her speed.

"C'mon, Flash, take it home!" shouted Margaret.

"Come on, Flash! Come on, Flash!" the crowd chanted.

With the fat end of her bat Sophie tapped the dirt from her spikes.

Margaret looked out at the pitcher's mound. Millie Deegan had a wicked sidearm pitch. She rocked back on her right foot, lifted her left leg, and burned in a fastball. Sophie let it pass without swinging.

"Ball one!" The umpire pointed a finger to the sky.

"Good eye, Sophie," encouraged Margaret's mother.

Margaret saw Millie wipe the sweat from her forehead on her sleeve. Then, without hesitating, she fired in a perfect pitch.

Whack! The sound of Sophie's wooden bat connecting with the ball broadcast the glorious news of a hit. It shot into left field like an arrow sure of its target. Sophie charged toward first base.

"Safe!" called the umpire.

The crowd shouted its approval.

Margaret marked another "1" on her scorecard next to Sophie's name.

"Who's up next?" her father asked.

"'Moe' Trezza," she answered.

When Betty Trezza first joined the Belles, she had trouble remembering her teammates' names. When she wanted someone, she would yell "Moe!" to get their attention. As a friendly joke her teammates now called her "Moe." So did the fans.

"Go-o-O-O-O, Moe!" yelled Margaret. She crossed her fingers, hoping for a hit. Her eyes darted from Moe to Sophie and back again. Moe gripped the bat and peered out at the pitcher. Sophie crouched like a panther, leading off first base. She brushed the bill of her cap.

"That's a signal," Margaret whispered excitedly.

"This is it," said her mother.

Sophie tore off toward second base. Millie launched the pitch. Moe stood without moving a muscle and watched the ball sail by her. By the time it landed in the catcher's mitt, The Flash had stolen second.

Margaret and Robert leaped to their feet and cheered along with the other fans.

Stealing bases was not only legal, it was Sophie's specialty. This was her fifth stolen base of the night. Sophie had stolen 201 bases that season, an all-time, big-league record.

Dorothy Green, the catcher, threw the ball back to Millie. Millie straightened her cap, and slowly turned the ball over in her glove.

"What is she waiting for?" Margaret asked.

"She's pretending not to pay attention," said her father.

"But she really wants Sophie to try to steal again," added her mother. "And this time Millie hopes to pick her off with a throw to third."

"Sophie, be careful," Margaret whispered, and slipped her hand into her mother's. She looked back at Moe, who choked up on the bat as if to bunt. The infielders drew in close.

Millie checked Sophie on second. Then she curled her pitching arm, and as her hand came level with her waist, she snapped her wrist. The ball zoomed toward home plate.

Crack! Moe's bat connected with the ball and fooled everyone with a grounder. It skimmed along the grass into right field like a skipping stone thrown across a pond.

The right fielder raced forward and scooped up the ball. Moe landed safely at first. Sophie touched third, but she didn't stop there. She flew on toward home plate.

"Go, Flash, go!" screamed Margaret.

"Go, Flash, go!" screamed the crowd.

Sophie streaked along the base path. Her spikes pounded the earth. The dust flew. Close behind her was the throw from right field.

"Hurry, Sophie!" shouted Margaret.

If the throw got to home plate before Sophie, and the catcher tagged her, Sophie would be out.

The catcher yanked off her mask to see the incoming ball more clearly. With one foot on home, she snatched the ball out of the air and reached out to tag Sophie.

Sophie hit the dirt on her side. Sliding feet-first, she hooked her left leg and scraped the corner of home plate with her toe. She was home free, out of the catcher's reach. She had brought in the winning run.

"Safe!" yelled the umpire.

The air exploded with hoots and roars and shouts.

Margaret's mother stuck two fingers in her mouth and let out a whistle. Her father whooped, and twirled an imaginary lariat. Margaret threw her cap in the air. Robert swung his jacket above his head. The sky rained scorecards and caps and hats. Margaret and Robert hugged their parents. The bleachers became a tangle of arms as fans in the row above reached down to join the embrace and fans in the row below reached up. Margaret didn't know any of these people, but she hugged them back.

Sophie's teammates poured out of the dugout and lifted her up onto their shoulders. It felt like the last day of school, the Fourth of July, the end of the War.

Margaret quickly marked the winning run on her scorecard and handed it to her father.

"You keep this one, Champ!" he yelled.

The family rushed onto the field with the other fans, chanting,
"So-phie! So-phie!" They pushed through the crush of people until they
neared her. Margaret's father motioned for her to climb up on his
shoulders.

"How do you feel?" a reporter called to Sophie above the noise.

"Wonderful!"

Margaret looked at Sophie's scraped and bloody knees, then at her own. You do have to be tough to play baseball in a skirt, she thought. She flashed a "V" for Victory and began to chant again, "So-phie! So-phie!"

# Rockford Peaches vs. Racine Belles
## Championship Game September 16, 1946

| Racine Belles | At-Bats | Runs | Hits | RBIs |
|---|---|---|---|---|
| Sophie Kurys, 2b . . . . . . . . . . . . . 5 | | 1 | 2 | 0 |
| Moe Trezza, ss . . . . . . . . . . . . . . 5 | | 0 | 1 | 1 |
| Pepper Paire, c . . . . . . . . . . . . . . 4 | | 0 | 0 | 0 |
| Edie Perlick, lf . . . . . . . . . . . . . . 5 | | 0 | 0 | 0 |
| Eleanor Dapkus, cf . . . . . . . . . . 5 | | 0 | 1 | 0 |
| Maddy English, 3b . . . . . . . . . . 5 | | 0 | 1 | 0 |
| Marnie Danhauser, 1b . . . . . . . . . 5 | | 0 | 0 | 0 |
| Betty Emry, rf . . . . . . . . . . . . . . 5 | | 0 | 0 | 0 |
| Joanne Winter, p . . . . . . . . . . . . 5 | | 0 | 0 | 0 |
| **Totals** | **44** | **1** | **5** | **1** |

| Rockford Peaches | At-Bats | Runs | Hits | RBIs |
|---|---|---|---|---|
| Dorothy Kamenshek, 1b . . . . . . . . 7 | | 0 | 4 | 0 |
| Dottie Ferguson, 2b . . . . . . . . . . 5 | | 0 | 2 | 0 |
| Lee Surkowski, cf . . . . . . . . . . . . 7 | | 0 | 1 | 0 |
| Naomi Meier, lf . . . . . . . . . . . . . 5 | | 0 | 2 | 0 |
| Dorothy Harrell, ss . . . . . . . . . . . 5 | | 0 | 1 | 0 |
| Rose Gacioch, rf . . . . . . . . . . . . . 6 | | 0 | 1 | 0 |
| Velma Abbott, 3b . . . . . . . . . . . . 7 | | 0 | 1 | 0 |
| Dorothy Green, c . . . . . . . . . . . . 5 | | 0 | 1 | 0 |
| Carolyn Morris, p . . . . . . . . . . . . 4 | | 0 | 0 | 0 |
| Mildred Deegan, p . . . . . . . . . . . 1 | | 0 | 0 | 0 |
| **Totals** | **52** | **0** | **13** | **0** |

| | | | | | | | |
|---|---|---|---|---|---|---|---|
| Rockford | 000 | 000 | 000 | 000 | 00—0 | 13 | 1 |
| Racine | 000 | 000 | 000 | 000 | 01—1 | 5 | 2 |

**Errors**—Abbott, Dapkus, English. **Left on base**—Rockford, 19; Racine, 6. **Triple**—Gacioch. **Stolen bases**—Kamenshek, Meier, Ferguson, Surkowski, Kurys (5), Winter. **Hit batters**—By Winter, Morris; by Morris, Trezza. **Time**—2:40. **Attendance**—5,630.

| Racine | Innings | Hits | Runs | Walks | Strikeouts |
|---|---|---|---|---|---|
| Winter, W | 14 | 13 | 0 | 4 | 4 |

| Rockford | Innings | Hits | Runs | Walks | Strikeouts |
|---|---|---|---|---|---|
| Morris | 11 | 3 | 0 | 1 | 8 |
| Deegan, L | 3 | 2 | 1 | 1 | 3 |

# AUTHORS' NOTE

Although Margaret and her family are fictitious characters, the details of the game are factual. The game took place on September 16, 1946, and has been re-created here through newspaper articles and interviews with Sophie Kurys, Betty Trezza, Joanne Winter, and Sue Macy. We thank these women for sharing their memories and their knowledge. We also appreciate the help of Bill Burdick and Tim Wiles of the National Baseball Hall of Fame, and Christopher Paulson of the Racine Heritage Museum. A special thanks to Stuart Rand of The Art of the Game, for the title.

During World War II (1939–1945), when American men went to battle, women filled their jobs at home. They worked in offices and factories building battleships and bombers—and they played baseball.

A women's baseball league was the idea of Philip Wrigley, the owner of the Chicago Cubs. He was worried that interest in baseball would not last through the war with so many outstanding male players fighting overseas. In 1943 he started a professional women's baseball league. Among the eight teams in the Midwest were the Racine Belles from Wisconsin and the Rockford Peaches from Illinois. In a grueling four-month season the women played one hundred and twenty games, one every night, with doubleheaders on Saturday or Sunday. At the end of each season the two best teams of the league competed for the championship.

When the war ended, the men came home and took back their former jobs in the factories, offices, and ballparks. Attendance at women's baseball games dropped and the league eventually folded in 1954. The accomplishments of these female athletes were largely forgotten.

In 1988 the Baseball Hall of Fame in Cooperstown, New York, acknowledged these amazing athletes in an exhibit. One hundred and forty-seven former players attended the opening of the "Women in Baseball" exhibit, along with hundreds of their friends, families, and fans. The names of six hundred and fifty women players in the league are listed in a glass case. As names of more players are discovered, they will be added to the roster.

The official name of the league changed many times. During the 1980's, former players renamed it the All-American Girls Professional Baseball League (AAGPBL). For reasons of simplicity and respect, we have chosen to use this name.

The Rockford Peaches, 1946. *Front row, left to right:* Betty Yahr, Dorothy Cook, Lee Surkowski, Helen Filarski, Olive Little, Marge Holgerson, Dorothy Harrell, Carolyn Morris. *Back row, left to right:* manager Bill Allington, Rose Gacioch, Dorothy Kamenshek, Dorothy Green, Dorothy Moon, Naomi Meier, Mildred Deegan, Helen Smith, Marge Wigiser, chaperone Mildred Lundahl. This photo was taken prior to Dottie Ferguson and Velma Abbott joining the team. (Courtesy of Clem Krivich.)

Members of the Music Maids in the National Girls Baseball League, 1951–1952. *Top row, left to right:* Edie Perlick, Maddy English, Joanne Winter. *Bottom row, left to right:* Betty Trezza, Sophie Kurys.

A recent photo of Sophie Kurys